Pee Wees
on Parade

Pee Wees on Parade

JUDY DELTON

Illustrated by Alan Tiegreen

A YOUNG YEARLING BOOK

For Joan King, who said rodeo to me,
and Dr. Bob Hasel and Lynn, who will
recognize my gold tooth

Published by
Dell Publishing
a division of
Bantam Doubleday Dell Publishing Group, Inc.
1540 Broadway
New York, New York 10036

ISBN: 0-440-40700-1

Printed in the United States of America

July 1992

10 9 8 7 6 5 4 3

CWO

Contents

CHAPTER 1

Ride 'Em, Cowboy

I t was Tuesday.

Tuesday was the meeting day for Pee Wee Scout Troop 23.

The Scouts poured out of cars.

Others jumped off their bikes.

They scrambled up Mrs. Peters's front steps.

"Have I got a surprise today!" said their leader.

The Scouts loved surprises. They followed Mrs. Peters down the basement steps to their meeting room.

"What is it?" asked Roger White, tipping

his chair back on two legs. "Is it something we'll like?"

"You'll love it!" said their leader.

"Roger is going to tip over backward," whispered Molly Duff to her best friend, Mary Beth Kelly.

Just as she said that, there was a loud crash.

Roger was on the floor. His chair was on top of him.

After Mrs. Peters helped him up, she said, "Remember when we got our Good Manners badge? What was one of the rules we learned then?"

"Don't chew with food in your mouth," shouted Tim Noon.

"Don't eat ice cream with a fork," cried Tracy Barnes.

Mrs. Peters frowned. The Scouts laughed.

Rachel Meyers's hand was waving.

"Yes, Rachel," said Mrs. Peters.

"Raise your hand when you want to

talk," said Rachel. "And don't tip on chairs."

"Smart aleck," said Roger to Rachel, rubbing his arm where it had hit the floor.

"That's right," said their leader. "Tipping on chairs can lead to accidents. It could be a bad accident," she added, frowning at Roger.

"Roger's such a show-off," said Mary Beth. "He does that to get attention. He probably fell on purpose."

Mary Beth was right, thought Molly. Once at a wedding he told Molly that they were married. He put a toy ring on her finger and called her Mrs. White. That was scary. Molly didn't want to be married. Not yet. And certainly not to Roger. If she married some-one in the Scout troop, it would be Kevin Moe. Molly liked Kevin. Kevin had plans. He wanted to be mayor when he grew up.

"Who knows what holiday is coming?" asked Mrs. Peters.

"Christmas?" said Tim.

All of the Scouts burst into laughter. Tim turned red.

"It's summer!" shouted Rachel. "How could it be Christmas in summer?"

Roger made a make-believe snowball and threw it at Tim.

Some of the other Pee Wees said "Ho ho ho!" like Santa Claus.

"Anyone can make a mistake," said Mrs. Peters, tapping on the table for silence.

"Do you know, Molly?" asked their leader.

Molly's hand wasn't up. But she knew that even teachers could call on you sometimes when your hand wasn't up. It was a trick to make sure you were listening.

"The Fourth of July?" asked Molly.

"That's right!" said Mrs. Peters. "It's the

birthday of our nation. And my good news is that the rodeo is coming to town for the holiday!"

The Scouts cheered. "Yeah!" they all shouted.

"What's a rodeo?" asked Lisa Ronning.

Some of the other Scouts looked puzzled too.

Rachel's hand was waving. "Can I tell them, Mrs. Peters?" she said.

Mrs. Peters nodded.

"A rodeo," said Rachel importantly, "is a roundup. Cowboys and horses come and do fancy riding and they lasso calves and ride bulls and get thrown off and there are contests and food and stuff."

"Real horses are coming?" asked Sonny Stone.

Sonny used to be Sonny Betz until his mother married the fire chief and now he was Sonny Stone. His mother was the assistant troop leader.

"No, dummy, artificial horses!" said Roger.

"There will be real horses," said Mrs. Peters, giving Roger a warning look.

The Pee Wees began to gallop around the room, pretending they were on horseback.

"Neeiigh," said Kevin, making a horsey sound through his nose.

"Giddyap!" shouted Kenny Baker, slapping his knee. Kenny was Patty Baker's twin brother.

"We never had a rodeo in town before," said Molly.

"I'm scared of horses," said Mary Beth. "They've got such big faces."

Molly tried to remember if she'd ever met a real horse. She had seen pictures of horses. Lots of pictures in her farm books. And she had seen horses in movies. Big brown horses with their hair flying in the breeze.

"They are big," said Molly. "I think they are very tall."

7

"Horses smell," said Lisa. "They smell like the circus."

"The circus smells like popcorn," said Mary Beth. "I think they smell like the animal barn at the state fair."

"They smell wonderful," said Rachel. "My cousin has a horse of her own."

Molly was glad that Mrs. Peters held up her hand again for quiet before Rachel could brag about knowing her cousin's horse.

"Horses are intelligent, sensitive animals," she said. "This is a perfect chance for you all to get to know about them firsthand. I have more news. The rodeo star, Mr. Glen Cooper, has asked us, the Pee Wee Scouts, to participate in the Fourth of July rodeo parade! We will all get to ride down Main Street on horseback!"

The whole Scout troop was stunned. They stared at Mrs. Peters.

The Pee Wees on horseback?

Molly began to feel a familiar feeling in her stomach.

It wasn't the flu but it was close. It was a scary feeling.

It came when she had to do something that she wasn't sure she could do. She had had it when she had to earn the Baby-Tending badge, and she had no baby to tend. All the other Scouts had brothers and sisters or at least relatives. Molly was an only child.

She had had the feeling when she had to skate and her skates were too tight.

And now she had it because she had no idea how to ride a horse. She had a feeling everyone in her troop would ride down Main Street but her.

"Now for the rest of the news!" said Mrs. Peters.

Was there more horsey news, thought Molly?

"I thought this was the perfect opportunity

for our troop to get our Horseback-Riding badge!" smiled Mrs. Peters. "The perfect chance for us to study horses and learn to ride."

It was worse than she thought! Not only did she have to ride a horse down Main Street so everyone could see her when she fell into the gutter, but now everyone would get a badge but her! This made the Baby-Tending badge look as easy as apple pie.

Rachel's hand was waving.

"Yes, Rachel?" said their leader.

"I took horseback-riding lessons," she said. "I can ride with a saddle, or bareback. I've got jodhpurs and everything. If you like, I can lead the parade."

Rat's knees! thought Molly. Rachel could twirl a baton. Rachel took ballet lessons. What couldn't she do?

"That's good news," said Mrs. Peters. "That means you can help some of the others who have never been on a horse."

"I'd be glad to, Mrs. Peters," said Rachel.

"Have you ever been on a horse?" whispered Molly to Mary Beth.

"Once," she said. "At my grandpa's farm. But I don't like horses. I'm afraid of them."

Rat's knees. Even Mary Beth had been on a horse. Her best friend. Everyone was talking about horses. And everyone was telling about how they galloped and trotted all over the place.

"I think some of them are lying," said Lisa. "I'll bet Sonny Stone can't ride a horse."

Lisa must be right. Sonny still had training wheels on his bike and he was seven years old.

But that didn't help Molly.

Was it possible to put training wheels on a horse?

She would have to think of something.

She wasn't going to be the only one without a Horseback-Riding badge!

CHAPTER 2

The Training Horse

"Now let's tell our good deeds that we've all done this week," said Mrs. Peters. "Then we can say our pledge and sing our Pee Wee Scout song, and eat our cupcakes."

The Scouts cheered. They all liked the cupcakes. That was one of the fun things about being Scouts. The food. Sometimes they had ice cream with the cupcakes.

Mrs. Peters got baby Nick up from his nap and brought him downstairs. Their mascot, Lucky, was there too. "Arf!" he said.

Just as they were about to tell their good deeds, Mrs. Stone came downstairs. She came to help Mrs. Peters. She had her two new adopted babies with her, Lee and Lani. Sonny left his chair and came over and sat on his mother's lap.

"What a baby," said Rachel.

"I think Mrs. Stone has three babies instead of two," said Lisa.

"Sonny is still jealous," said Molly. "It isn't easy getting a new dad and a brother and sister all at once."

Molly felt sorry for Sonny. She didn't like it when the Scouts laughed at him.

"Now the good deeds!" said Mrs. Peters.

Hands waved in the air.

"I helped my dad change the oil in his car," said Roger without waiting to be called on.

"I'll bet he was a big help," said Tracy. "He probably handed him the oil can."

"I fed my baby cousin her strained peas," said Rachel. "And she doesn't like them. I made train noises and my aunt says

she's going to hire me to feed her all the time."

"La de dah," said Roger.

"Hey, Patty Cake," said Roger to Patty. "What did you do?"

Patty turned red. Roger and Patty liked each other.

"I planted asparagus for my mom," she said. "In the garden."

Roger made choking and gagging noises.

"Yuck," said Sonny. "I hate asparagus."

"It's good for you," said Kenny.

"Molly?" asked Mrs. Peters. "Did you do any good deeds this week?"

Molly had had a good deed ready. But now she forgot. She tried to think, but nothing came to her mind.

"I forgot," she said.

"Ha, you didn't do any," said Roger.

"Did too," said Molly.

"Did not, did not, it's a lie, your tongue is hot," said Roger.

16

"I did a good deed," Molly whispered to Mary Beth. "I just can't think of it."

Mary Beth believed her. She was a good friend.

"I cleaned my mom's silver, too," said Rachel.

Rat's knees. Rachel had two good deeds.

"I wiped Jell-O up off the kitchen floor," said Tim.

"I gave Lani a bottle," said Sonny.

Mary Beth had baby-sat her little sister.

Tim had petted a stray cat.

Molly's mother didn't like her to pet stray animals.

After all the good deeds were told, the Scouts made a big circle. They all joined hands. Then they sang their song.

Molly liked it when they sang. She felt like the Scouts were a big family. It made her feel warm and cozy inside.

They sang to the tune of "Old MacDonald Had a Farm":

17

Scouts are helpers, Scouts have fun,
Pee Wee, Pee Wee Scouts!
We sing and play when work is done,
Pee Wee, Pee Wee Scouts!

With a good deed here,
And an errand there,
Here a hand, there a hand,
Everywhere a good hand.

Scouts are helpers, Scouts have fun,
Pee Wee, Pee Wee Scouts!

After the song they said their pledge:

We love our country
And our home,
Our school and neighbors too.

As Pee Wee Scouts
We pledge our best
In everything we do.

Molly almost got tears in her eyes, it sounded so good to her.

The troop went outside and played a few yard games.

Nick and Lucky played too.

Molly almost forgot about the rodeo. About the horses. But when the meeting was just about over, Mrs. Peters said, "Boys and girls, next meeting I am taking you to the Lucky Bow Ranch, where we will all watch the ranchers mount their horses and ride. The owner will give us some tips about horses and their habits and how to ride one. Isn't that exciting news? I saved the best till last!"

"I already know how to ride, Mrs. Peters," said Rachel. "Should I just stay home next Tuesday?"

"No, Rachel, we can all learn something, even experts," said their leader.

Rachel nodded and sighed. "It will be boring," she said.

It would not be boring for Molly.

On the way home, Mary Beth said, "I don't want to go."

"Neither do I," cried Molly.

"But then we won't get our badge. And we won't be able to be in the parade," said Mary Beth.

None of the other Scouts seemed worried.

Kevin pretended he was on horseback all the way home.

"I think I'm allergic to horses," said Tracy. "I hope my mom lets me go."

"I hope my mom doesn't," said Mary Beth. "Fat chance."

"I'm going to see if I can go out to the farm and practice riding before next week," said Lisa. "Then I won't be so rusty."

"We have to practice too!" said Molly to Mary Beth. "We can't be the only dummies."

"On what?" said Mary Beth.

The two girls sat down on a park bench to think.

21

"On something smaller than a horse," said Molly.

"We've got a sawhorse in our garage," said Mary Beth. "I'm not afraid to ride that."

Molly shook her head. "That doesn't move," she said. "Anybody can ride a little old sawhorse."

The girls thought some more.

"A dog might be good," said Mary Beth. "But Skippy is too little. We'd squish her flat if we sat on her back."

Molly snapped her fingers. "Mrs. Wicks's dog!" she said. "He always gives little kids a ride. Jules is a great big Saint Bernard! He'd be good to start with, then you'd get over being scared of horses!"

Mary Beth looked doubtful. But Molly jumped up and pulled her down the street toward Jules's house.

When they got there, Mrs. Wicks wasn't home, but Jules was in the yard guarding the house. He gave the girls a big lick.

"He's huge!" cried Mary Beth.

He looked huge to Molly, too, but she said, "Pooh. He's perfect for a beginning horse. Aren't you, Jules?"

"Woof!" said Jules. He looked as if he were smiling. He looked as if he would love to give the girls a ride.

"How do we get on him?" said Mary Beth. "We need those stirrups."

"Naw," said Molly. "We just swing our leg over his back."

Molly held on to Jules's collar. She swung her leg over his back. Jules thought she was playing. He dashed out from under her and rolled over on his back.

"Come on, boy!" said Mary Beth. "We can't ride you if you're lying down!"

"It will be easier to get on him when he's lower," said Molly.

As soon as Jules turned over, Molly sat on his back. When he stood up, her feet did not touch the ground.

"Look!" she said. "I'm riding him!"

But Molly spoke too soon. Jules saw a squirrel and leapt after him. When he leapt ahead, Molly slid over his smooth hair and down over his tail to the ground.

"I can't even ride a dog!" she cried. "How am I ever going to ride a real horse?"

Mary Beth tried next. Jules walked about two feet before he had an itch and sat down to scratch with his back leg. Mary Beth slid off and onto the ground.

"He's slippery," said Mary Beth. "I think he needs a saddle."

The girls petted Jules's head. He wagged his big tail.

"You're a good dog, Jules," said Molly. "But you are no horse."

The girls waved to their steed, and started walking home.

CHAPTER 3
Ten-Gallon Hat

When Molly got home, she remembered the good deed. She had helped her dad clean up the yard. While he raked she'd picked up sticks and gum wrappers and newspapers that had blown into the yard.

"Rat's knees!" she said out loud. "Why didn't I think of it when I needed it?"

Maybe she could use it next time. She'd try to remember it by thinking that *rake* rhymed with *bake* and *bake* rhymed with *cake* and cake was something they would have at the rodeo. And she couldn't forget the rodeo.

But maybe they wouldn't have cake at the

rodeo. Maybe she should remember that *rake* rhymed with *break*, which is what might happen to her legs and arms if she didn't learn to ride a horse.

That was too scary. She would remember her good deed by rhyming *yard* with *hard*. It would be hard to ride a horse. And she could not forget the word *horse*.

"A rodeo is coming to town," she announced at dinner that evening.

"I heard about that," said Mrs. Duff. "I hear the Pee Wees are going to ride on horseback down Main Street in the parade."

"Good for you," said Mr. Duff, taking some more mashed potatoes and gravy. "I'll bet you'll be on TV."

Weren't her parents even worried about their young daughter on horseback? Didn't they remember that the only horse she'd ever been on had been on the merry-go-round at the circus? They didn't even seem to care.

"Please pass the pork chops," said Mrs. Duff to her husband.

"What's for dessert?" asked Molly's father.

Then her parents began a discussion of how to make Blueberry Delight, instead of giving Molly some tips on horses.

"It's perfectly easy," her mother was saying.

"Riding a horse?" asked Molly.

Her mother laughed. "No, making this dessert," she said.

After dinner Molly helped her father clear the table and do the dishes. There was no horse talk. Just calorie talk.

When she finished the dishes, Molly went into the living room and turned on the TV. There was a western movie on. There were horses in the movie. There was a rodeo in the movie!

Molly turned the sound up. There was a cowboy on a bucking bronco! She watched as the cowboy hung on.

The horse reared.

His front feet were in the air.

The cowboy slid to one side.

Then he slid to the other side.

Then he slid up the neck of the horse.

And then he slid backward and onto the ground.

Into the dust.

Two men had to carry him off the field. People cheered but the cowboy looked dazed.

Molly turned off the TV and ran upstairs to call Mary Beth.

"We might have to ride a bucking bronco!" she told her. "We might get a horse that tries to throw us off!"

"I'm not going," said Mary Beth. "I'm not going to go to the Fourth of July rodeo. And that's that."

"Rat's knees," said Molly. "You have to get your badge. Do you want to be the only one without a horse badge?"

Mary Beth thought about that. It was definitely no fun to be the only Scout without a badge.

"Well, you and Sonny," added Molly.

Mary Beth didn't want to be a baby like Sonny.

"We have to go," said Molly, sadly.

The next Tuesday the Pee Wees met at Mrs. Peters's house.

Most of them had jeans on. Sonny had overalls with straps. And Rachel had her riding outfit on. She had jodhpurs and a black coat and black riding hat that looked like a bonnet, Molly thought.

They got into Mrs. Peters's van and started for the Lucky Bow Ranch. When they got there, the owner, Mr. Granger, met them.

"Welcome to the Lucky Bow," he said.

Mr. Granger had jeans on. And a blue shirt with a string tie like the cowboys on TV wore. He had on real cowboy boots with

pictures carved in them, and spurs on the heels.

"He's got a ten-gallon hat!" said Roger. "That's what they call those things."

Mr. Granger's hat did look like it would hold ten gallons of something. It was huge. The man's face was red and ruddy. He looked like he had been out on the range in the hot sun.

"He's bowlegged," whispered Tracy. "That's what happens when you ride a horse too long."

"Does not," snapped Rachel. "I ride a horse and I am not bowlegged."

Rachel made a point of standing with her knees close together.

Mr. Granger and his ranchers took the Scouts to a large fenced-in area where horses were munching grass.

"Now, how many of you have been on a horse before?" he asked.

Hands waved. Rachel's. Sonny's.

"Hey, when have you been on a horse?" Roger asked Sonny.

"I have," said Sonny.

"Yeah, a rocking horse!" snorted Roger.

"I've been on a grocery store horse," said Sonny.

Roger bent over in laughter. "You mean the one you put a dime in?" he hooted.

One by one the men got on the horses to show the Pee Wees how it was done. They showed them how to get on and how to get off. They showed them how to sit in the saddle. And how to use the reins. Then they showed them how they rounded up cattle.

"This is a lasso," said Mr. Granger. "Sometimes called a lariat."

He twirled a long rope over his head and around and around in a circle. As the children watched, he lassoed a fence post and tightened the noose in the rope.

"Now, if I was trying to get one of the

cows, that would go around his neck," he said. "It wouldn't hurt him, it would just guide him back to the herd."

The Pee Wees grabbed their own necks and pretended there was a rope around them. They gagged and choked until Mrs. Peters had to clap her hands.

"I wouldn't want that old rope around my neck," said Patty.

"Our necks aren't thick like cows'," said Kenny. "Cows are tough."

Mr. Granger passed the lasso around the group. He let each Scout try to lasso the post with it.

"Get a good spin on it first," he said. "In the air."

The Pee Wees all tried hard. They wanted to lasso the imaginary cow.

Roger lassoed a bush.

"Ho ho ho!" laughed the Scouts.

"Just wait," he said. "You can't do any better."

He was right.

Tracy lassoed some blades of grass.

Tim lassoed an old shoe.

Mary Beth missed the fence post by ten feet.

Molly kept moving to the end of the line so she wouldn't have to have a turn. It was a bad enough worry to stay on a horse. She didn't want to fail at this too.

Even Mrs. Peters couldn't hook the fence post.

Rachel came close.

And Kevin was the only one to do it!

"Yeah!" shouted the troop.

Molly flushed with pride. Kevin was smart. He could do anything. He would make a wonderful mayor. And he was Molly's boyfriend! He was the man Molly was going to marry someday! Even if he didn't know it yet.

"Now," said Mr. Granger. "Who would like to take a ride on the back of Sally?"

Everyone's hand went up except Molly's and Mary Beth's.

Sonny waved his hand hardest of all.

"He's too dumb to know he can't ride," said Roger. "He'll be off that horse in a flash."

But Sonny didn't fall off.

Mr. Granger led Sally up to Sonny.

"That old nag sags in the middle," shouted Roger. "She's a swayback."

Mr. Granger patted Sally on the head. "She's a very gentle animal," he said. "She's old and she's slow and she's a Shetland pony."

A pony! If this was a pony, why was it so *big*? thought Molly. Sally looked like a horse to Molly.

Two ranchers helped Sonny put a foot in the stirrup. Then one helped boost him up into the saddle. He was just about to slide over the pony and down the other side, but the man on the other side grabbed him. Then

the men adjusted Sonny's stirrups and handed him a rope that looked like the reins. The men held on to Sonny, and Sally walked a few feet very very slowly.

"He's not really holding the reins," said Rachel. "He's holding a rope that doesn't go anywhere. That man is holding the reins."

"And they're holding him in the saddle!" scoffed Roger. "He couldn't fall off that nag if he tried! He looks like a baby stuck in a car seat!"

"We can't be too careful the first time," said Mrs. Peters, glaring at Roger.

Sally and the two men and Sonny walked around in a circle. Slowly. Then they lifted Sonny down off the pony.

"Hey," he said. "I didn't fall off! I can ride a horse!"

Molly stamped her foot. He was right. Car seat or not, Sonny rode the horse. Even Sonny could say he had ridden a real horse now. A horse that wasn't a grocery store mechanical horse. Or a merry-go-round horse. He was braver than Molly. And he had not fallen off.

Roger rode next.

"I want the real reins," he said. "And I can get on this little pony myself."

Roger did get on himself. But he landed facedown in the saddle! The men grabbed him and set him up and straightened him out.

"Giddyap!" said Roger, slapping the reins on Sally's neck. Sally didn't move. "Giddyap!" he said again. Sally stood still and looked bored.

It was only when the ranchers began to walk alongside Sally that she moved.

"I don't know if I can ride a pony," said Rachel. "I usually have a big spunky horse."

Rachel really did get on Sally all alone. She swung her leg over the saddle and landed straight and tall. Her feet stayed in the stirrups, and Sally walked along smartly after Rachel said a few nice words to her.

"She knows how to talk to horses," said Mary Beth with admiration.

"She's had lessons," scoffed Sonny.

"Can she gallop?" asked Rachel. "Or even trot?"

"Not this time," said Mrs. Peters quickly.

Rachel dismounted and sighed. She brushed off her jodhpurs and removed her hat.

"That was so boring," she announced.

It took a long time for the Scouts to have a turn on Sally. Molly and Mary Beth stayed at the end of the line. Before long, Mrs. Peters looked at her watch and said, "Dear me, it is four o'clock already! Time for us to leave."

"But Mrs. Peters, Molly and Mary Beth didn't get a turn!" shouted Rachel. "That's not fair."

"Yes, it is," said Molly quickly. "We don't mind, do we, Mary Beth?"

40

Mary Beth shook her head. "We don't mind."

"That is a shame," said Mrs. Peters.

"I guess we moved a little too slow," said Mr. Granger. "You can come back again soon," he added, waving his ten-gallon hat.

"Not on your life," whispered Mary Beth.

"That's right," whispered Molly. "We got as close to a horse today as I want to get."

But down deep Molly couldn't help remembering that Sonny had ridden a horse and she had not.

"You'll all get your turn," said Mrs. Peters sweetly, "on the Fourth of July. You'll each have your very own horse to ride in the parade!"

CHAPTER 4

Sonny's Important Job

"**M**rs. Peters!" called Molly when everyone was getting out of the van. "We forgot to tell our good deeds today!"

"Next week," said Mrs. Peters. "Today there is no time. Just hold on to it till next Tuesday, Molly."

Rat's knees, thought Molly. She hoped she could remember it till then. Cake, bake— what was the deed that rhymed?

"Did you have fun at the OK Corral?" asked Molly's dad, walking like a cowboy and clamping an imaginary hat on his head.

"Yes," Molly lied.

"Good," said her mother. "We have to start thinking of what you'll wear in the parade."

The next week flew by. Molly got books out of the library about horses. Most of them told what they ate and how to care for them instead of how to stay on top of them.

The next Tuesday the Pee Wees rushed to their meeting. Most of them couldn't wait to talk about the rodeo.

"I brought my blue ribbons I won for riding," said Rachel. She held up blue ribbons with gold writing on them. Everyone gathered around her except Molly. Even Mary Beth went to look.

"Rat's knees," said Molly. "I'll never get a blue ribbon."

"I just hope we get a badge," said Mary Beth.

"Mrs. Peters," called Rachel. "My mom says it's okay if I lead the Pee Wees on horseback. She'll sign the papers that say it's okay if I fall off. She knows I won't," she added.

"If you like, Mrs. Peters, I can lead the parade on horseback and twirl my baton at the same time," Rachel went on.

"Well, we'll think about that," said Mrs. Peters, not saying yes or no to Rachel's offer.

"Right now we have something else to discuss. Today we are going to clean up the park for the rodeo."

It looked like their leader was not going to ask for good deeds today, thought Molly.

"We'll pick up trash and weed the flower beds," she said. "We might even help paint the bandstand. It is the perfect chance for us to help others."

The Pee Wees cheered. They dashed out to Mrs. Peters's van.

When they got to the park, some workers had rakes and tools ready for them. A city truck was there with paint and other supplies.

First the Scouts got plastic bags and picked up trash that had blown around from picnics and parties. There were paper plates and cups. And paper bags and old food and soda cans. Molly even found an old sneaker someone had lost.

Then the Scouts raked.

Then they planted flowers.

Molly worked hard. So did Kevin and Kenny and Mary Beth and Rachel.

"Roger doesn't do any work," said Tracy. "He's just goofing around."

Roger was chasing Sonny with something from the trash.

"It's a dead squirrel!" he called to scare him.

"It's a dead rag," said Mary Beth in disgust.

Mrs. Peters clapped her hands. "Boys!" she called. "We are here to work!" She took

45

Roger's "dead squirrel" from him and put it in the trash. Mary Beth was right. It was a rag.

Sonny came and sat down on a rock. "Nobody lets me do anything important," he said. "I always do stuff that's easy."

"That's because you're such a baby," said Roger.

Molly wished she could give Sonny something important to do. Maybe he was right. Maybe if people didn't treat him like a baby, he would grow up.

Mrs. Peters must have thought the same thing.

She put her hand on his shoulder.

"I have something important for you to do," she said.

Sonny's face brightened.

"We are going to help the other volunteers paint the bandstand," she said. "You can walk over to the truck and carry the paint over here."

"Me too!" shouted Roger.

"Can we help?" asked Tracy.

"No, this is Sonny's important job," said Mrs. Peters. "He can do it by himself. He can bring one can at a time very carefully," she added clearly.

The truck was only a short way away. The cans of paint were in the back. Molly could see them from where the Scouts stood. It looked like it would be hard for Sonny to make a mistake. This would be a chance for Sonny to prove himself!

Sonny walked over to the truck with his shoulders back. He turned around to be sure everyone was watching him. Then he took one can down by the handle. Then another. He carried two cans at once.

"One at a time," called Mrs. Peters.

"I can carry two!" bragged Sonny.

"Rat's knees!" said Molly, stamping her foot. "Why doesn't he listen?"

Sonny carried two cans at a time. He set

them down proudly in front of Mrs. Peters. Then he went back and got the other two.

Molly sighed. He had not dropped them.

One of the volunteer men named Ed opened the cans. He poured a little paint into pails for the Pee Wees.

"We'll do the high part," he said. "The Pee Wees can paint this important part next to the steps here."

"That isn't an important part," whispered Rachel. "It's a little teensy part that won't show."

Mrs. Peters gave the Pee Wees each a brush. She and Ed's wife stood over them so that they wouldn't paint each other.

"Who chose yellow for the bandstand?" asked Ed, looking at the paint.

"The city parks department," replied Mrs. Peters. She looked at the cans. They did not have labels. "Maybe I'd better check with the workers to be sure," she said.

But the workers were not in the truck.

"I guess they've gone on their break," said Ed. "They did say the paint would be on the truck."

Mrs. Peters nodded. Everyone began painting.

"It's a cheery color," said Patty. "It looks like daisies."

In a little while more painters came. Then Sonny's mother and his new father Larry, the fire chief, came to help. Sonny told them about his important job.

"Good for you!" said Larry, patting him on the back.

With so many painters, the bandstand was finished in no time.

"It's surely brighter than before," said Mary Beth.

"I thought bandstands were supposed to be white," said Molly.

The volunteers gathered up the equipment.

They cleaned the brushes.

They washed out the pails.

"Thanks to the Pee Wee Scouts for their help!" said Ed when they left.

When the Scouts got to Mrs. Peters's house, she and Mrs. Stone and Larry helped them wash up. Then they sang their song and started for home.

Molly tumbled into bed right after supper. It had been a busy day working in the park.

Just after dark she heard the telephone ring.

"Really?" her mother said. "Why, how could that have happened?"

There was silence while her mother was listening.

Molly got up and leaned over the banister in the hall.

"Oh, my goodness!" her mother exclaimed. "That is terrible! Are they blaming poor Sonny for this?"

Molly was wide-awake now. What happened? Was something the Pee Wees'

fault? Had Sonny done something to get them all in trouble? Something he'd have to go to jail for?

Molly forgot all about her horse worries. She forgot about her good deeds. From the sound of her mother's voice, there was a new worry even worse than those!

CHAPTER **5**

The Giant Green Raincoat

Molly heard her mother hang up the phone.

She heard her say something to her dad in a whisper.

Something about Sonny.

Something about after dark.

Something about Mrs. Peters, and the Pee Wees!

What could it be? Molly tossed and turned in bed. She couldn't go to sleep. She didn't want to let her mother know she had listened, or that she had leaned over the banister even though it was late at night.

54

Maybe there would be no rodeo! Maybe Rachel wouldn't get to lead the parade at all! Maybe the whole Pee Wee Scout troop would be in jail!

Every time Molly dozed off, she dreamed an awful dream. A dream like a nightmare. What had happened after dark that was so scary?

Finally morning came and Molly dashed downstairs to find out.

But before she could ask any questions, the phone rang. It was for her.

"Molly?" said Rachel. "Did you hear the news? Sonny is in real trouble!"

How did Rachel find out everything so fast?

"What happened?" Molly asked.

Rachel was glad to tell her.

"Last night," said Rachel, "Mr. Stone went back to the park to get some tools we forgot. It was real dark, but guess what?"

"What?" shouted Molly. It took Rachel

forever to get to the point when she was telling a story.

"The paint we painted the bandstand with wasn't yellow!"

"It was too, I saw it!" said Molly.

"Well, it is in the *daytime*," Rachel said. "But at night it lights up! It's a bright neon green, like chartreuse. You know, like those chartreuse socks I have that are called electric green?"

"Why would they want us to paint the bandstand electric green like your socks?" asked Molly.

"Well, they didn't," blurted Rachel. "Sonny took the wrong paint off the truck! That was the paint for highway signs, so people could read them at night! You know, the stuff they paint curbs and airport runways with so they will light up at night."

So Sonny was in trouble, just as she had thought. Big trouble. Poor Sonny, thought

Molly. His one important thing to do and he had failed.

"Well, it really wasn't Sonny's fault," said Molly. "Mrs. Peters told him to get it."

"Yes, but there was other paint on the truck right beside it that had a big sign on it. It said 'bandstand' big as life. It was white. The workman showed Larry the sign. It was huge. There wasn't any sign or any label on the stuff that lit up."

"Rat's knees!" said Molly. "I can't see how they can blame us."

"Not us—Sonny," said Rachel. "Well, I have to go and call the others. We're going out to watch the bandstand light up tonight, my dad and I," said Rachel. "Bye now."

Molly hung up.

"Will Sonny go to jail?" Molly asked her mother.

"Of course not," said her mother. "I still say it isn't Sonny's fault. He did what he was told."

"Well, he could have read that big sign," admitted Mr. Duff. "It was right in front of him."

Molly wondered if Sonny could read the word *bandstand*. He was pretty smart, but he didn't pay attention to things. He had a short attention span, their teacher at school said. The same teacher who said that Molly had a wild imagination. Molly had to admit she was probably right.

All day long the phone rang. The Scouts discussed the big mistake. Sonny's big mistake.

"We're going out to look at the bandstand tonight, do you want to come?" asked Mary Beth.

Molly ran to ask her parents. "Her dad is taking us," said Molly.

"Fine," said Mr. Duff. He trusted the Kellys.

That night it was not only Molly and the Kellys and Meyerses who were in the park.

All the Scouts and their relatives and friends were there! Mr. and Mrs. Peters were there too.

Molly could see the bandstand even before they got there. There was a sort of green glow in the sky. When they got closer, it was even brighter.

It reminded Molly of her glow-in-the-dark raincoat. It was yellow, but after dark, or in the closet, it glowed this same color green. Her mother said it was for safety, so if it was a dark rainy day, people in cars could see her crossing the street.

The bandstand was one great big giant green raincoat! But bandstands did not cross the street. They did not need this safety measure.

"Where's Sonny?" asked Roger.

"Roger wants to laugh at him," said Mary Beth. "He wants to scare him and tell Sonny he has to go to jail."

The Stones weren't there.

"They have to get the babies to bed early," said Mrs. Peters.

But the Pee Wees knew the real reason they didn't come.

"Ha," said Roger. "He's afraid to show up, that's the reason."

Mrs. Peters glared at Roger. Even in the dark Molly knew she was glaring.

"Well, I know one good thing," said Molly. "They won't need lights on for the band concerts. They can save on light bulbs this way."

Molly wanted to say something good about Sonny's mistake.

Some of the adults laughed politely about the light bulbs. Molly had not meant it to be a joke. They really did not need lights now.

"Hey," said Kevin to Molly. "The mayor is here! He's standing right behind you!"

The mayor walked to the bandstand. The paint was dry. Bright and dry. He stood on the top step to speak to the people. The glow of the neon green made the mayor's face look green too.

Molly wondered if he was going to arrest Sonny. Or make them paint the thing over and bill Sonny for all the paint. But instead he said, "I like it! As one little girl in the crowd said, we can save on light bulbs this way."

"That's you!" said Kevin, pointing. Everyone looked at Molly. She turned bright red. But it was too dark to notice.

"The bandstand will have to be painted white later," the mayor went on. "But for now I think we should leave it this way. It may give us a lot of publicity. It may put our town on the map. People may come from all over to listen to our concerts in the park and see the stand that lights up at night without light bulbs. I'll bet there isn't another like it for miles around!"

The applause was thunderous.

Molly couldn't believe her ears! Sonny's

mistake may have turned into something good! What was that called?

"Serendipity," said Rachel, as if she had read Molly's mind. "That's when something bad becomes something good unexpectedly."

"You know it would be a fine thing if it brought more people to the rodeo on the Fourth of July," said Mr. Kelly to Mrs. Peters.

"Yes, it would," said Mrs. Peters. "It is like free advertising."

Molly had mixed feelings. She was glad business would be good, but she didn't want any more people to see her fall off a horse on the holiday.

"Hi," said a voice behind Molly. It was Sonny! How did he hear the good news so fast?

"I came with my dad," said Sonny. "My mom couldn't wake the babies."

Roger began to chant, "Sonny, Sonny, he's all right!"

The crowd picked it up and chanted along with him.

Mr. Peters hoisted Sonny on his shoulders and walked through the crowd.

Molly was glad Roger didn't pick on Sonny. She was glad he praised him. It was time something nice happened to Sonny. Maybe Roger had a good side to him, too, thought Molly, even though it didn't show very often.

Sonny's important thing went from good to bad to good overnight. That was real serendipity, or else it was just plain good luck!

Now that Sonny's problem was solved, Molly's mind raced back to her horseback-riding worry. The Fourth of July was getting closer and closer, and Molly didn't know any more about horseback riding than she had when Mrs. Peters told them about the badge. Why didn't any of the Pee Wees except her (and Mary Beth) seem to worry? If only they gave badges for who could worry the most, Molly would be the winner!

CHAPTER 6

The Rodeo Star

Whizzzzz. Bang! A loud noise woke Molly up early on the Fourth of July. She jumped out of bed and ran to the window. She was just in time to see Roger dash around the corner of the house and down the street. When Molly opened the window, the air smelled like firecrackers!

The firecrackers reminded Molly of what day it was. The day reminded her of the rodeo. And the rodeo reminded her of horses.

Molly could hear her mother down in the kitchen making a Fourth of July breakfast.

Her dad was singing "Yankee Doodle" a little off-key.

Molly got dressed and went down to breakfast. Her mother put a piece of French toast shaped like a star on her plate.

"Eat a good breakfast," said Mrs. Duff. "You'll need your strength for the big day ahead."

Molly didn't feel like eating, but she ate anyway. Then it was time to leave for Mrs. Peters's house. She met Mary Beth on the way.

"I'm not afraid of horses anymore," she said to Molly. "My dad said these are little ponies not much bigger than a dog."

Pony-schmony, thought Molly. A pony was not a dog. A pony was a horse. And now Molly was the only one who couldn't ride one.

When they got there, everyone piled into the Peters's van and off they went. They passed the park where the band was playing.

The park was where the parade would start. But first they had to go to the fairgrounds to meet Glen Cooper, the rodeo star.

Mr. Peters parked the van, and the Scouts tumbled out and ran to a white fence that circled a big field. In the field were cowboys on horseback. Some were lassoing calves. Some were trying to stay on the backs of big brown horses. One cowboy was at the edge of the field grooming his horse with a big brush.

"He's currying his horse," said Rachel. "Look how shiny he is."

A man came running across the field with a shirt on that sparkled.

"His shirt has diamonds on it!" said Lisa.

"They are sequins," said Mrs. Peters. "It is a fancy rodeo shirt."

"I'm Glen Cooper," said the sparkly man with a big smile. He held out his hand to the

Scouts. "And you must be the Pee Wee Scouts."

"He has a southern drawl," said Rachel. "Lots of cowboys do."

"Isn't he handsome?" whispered Lisa. "Look at his big muscles!"

"She's boy crazy," whispered Tracy.

This was no boy, thought Molly. This was a grown man that Lisa was admiring!

Lisa was gazing up into Glen's smiling tan face. He had one gold tooth that shone in the sun as brightly as the sequins on his shirt.

"He's probably got a wife and lots of kids," said Tracy to Lisa.

Molly wondered what difference that made. He couldn't be the boyfriend of someone seven years old! He was an old man! Glen must be twenty years old, thought Molly.

"I hear you all want to ride in the parade," said Glen. "You want to be my help-ers?"

All the Scouts shouted *yes* except Molly. She said *no,* but no one heard her.

The Pee Wees stood and watched the men on horseback. Glen rode best of all. He was the star of the rodeo.

Across from the field there were booths set up that sold food and soft drinks. Some booths had games and contests. Molly's dad had given her spending money for the rodeo games.

People strolled over to watch the cowboys. Others began to play games at the booths.

"Mrs. Peters, can I try to get a ring around a horse's neck?" asked Sonny.

The horses were not real, Molly noticed. They were little metal horses in a booth. People were throwing rings to see if they could "lasso" one of them. In the back of the booth were shelves of things you could win. Big teddy bears with cowboy hats on. Stuffed horses with spangly saddles. And in the front, little tiny dogs.

Mrs. Peters led the Pee Wees over to the booth.

"Fifty cents, three for a dollar!" barked the man in the booth.

Mrs. Peters got three rings for each of the Pee Wees.

"Me first!" yelled Sonny. "I'm going to win one of those big horses!"

His first ring hit the back of the booth.

His second one fell on the floor.

And Sonny's third ring went out of the booth altogether and landed in a little boy's wagon that was going by!

Poor Sonny, thought Molly. But Mrs. Peters did not baby him.

"Next up!" she called, and Roger threw

one of his rings. His ring hit the horse and bounced off.

"They make them that way," said Kenny. "So they fall off. That way they don't have to give away those big prizes."

Roger's next ring went on the floor. But his third went around a horse's neck!

"I'll take that big bear with the hat," said Roger importantly.

But the man handed him a little dog.

"The bears are for three rings on," he said. "The horses are for two rings. And for one ring, you win a dog."

Roger stuffed the little dog in his pocket. He looked embarrassed.

"Good for you, Roger," said Mrs. Peters.

Most of the Scouts won nothing. Three of them won dogs. And then it was Molly's turn.

She closed one eye. She crossed her fingers. She used her left hand for luck. She said "Star light, star bright" because it made her wishes come true. She had played horseshoes with her cousins at picnics. This felt the same.

Swish! went the first ring. Right on the horse's neck!

Swish! went the second. Around the same horse!

And Swish! went the third. On the horse down at the end of the row.

"Yeah!" shouted the Pee Wees.

"Wow!" said Roger. "You are better than me!"

That took a lot of courage for Roger to say, thought Molly.

Even Sonny said, "Good for you."

Molly couldn't believe her luck.

"Choose a bear!" said Rachel.

Molly looked them all over. They all were big. And they all were soft and cuddly. They

all had big hats on, but they had different-color cowboy suits.

"I'll take the blue one," said Molly.

"It's as big as you are!" laughed Mrs. Peters. "If you get tired of carrying it, let me know. I'll carry it and everyone will think I won it!"

Everyone looked at Molly as they walked around the fairgrounds. Little children pointed. Adults turned their heads. Her mother and father were very surprised. It was fun to win at something. Now she wouldn't feel so bad about falling off her pony in the parade. Maybe she could get a badge for getting rings on the horse's neck!

Molly decided rodeos were fun.

Clowns came through doing somersaults.

Cowboys on ponies rode through, smiling.

Children ate pink cotton candy.

And music played all day.

At noon the Scouts sat under a shade tree and ate the sandwiches Mrs. Peters had brought. They lay on the soft grass and rested. And then the rodeo show began.

The Pee Wees got into their seats in the grandstand to watch.

But Molly couldn't keep her attention on the cowboys roping cows. She didn't want to look at the cowboys bursting out of swinging gates on horses that tried to throw them off.

"Yeah!" shouted the Pee Wees.

"Did you see that?" shouted Roger as one cowboy bounced to the ground and up onto his horse again.

Molly covered her eyes.

Finally Mrs. Peters said, "Now for the parade!"

The Scouts and Nick and Molly's rodeo bear all got into the van again and drove to the park. There were the horses that were called ponies, all lined up with bright colorful ornaments on their reins.

"I want the spotted one!" shouted Sonny, dashing ahead and climbing onto it.

Alongside the ponies were parents and helpers to help the Pee Wees onto their ponies and to walk beside them holding on to their saddles.

"Look, they are just like big doggies!" said Mary Beth, patting one on the nose.

"I never saw dogs with horseshoes on their feet!" said Molly.

The pony that Molly was to ride had a friendly face. His eyes looked warm and trusting. Molly thought, I can do this. But just when Molly was going to put her foot up into the stirrup and climb on his back, her pony shifted. He picked up one of his feet. And when he put it down, it was in a different place than it had been before. It was not on the ground. It was on Molly's foot!

Molly waited politely for her horse to move his foot. She waited and waited.

The other Pee Wees were on their ponies!

No one noticed that Molly could not move her foot. They were all watching Glen Cooper. The cowboy was at the head of the parade. His hands were in the air and his face was smiling. Smiling at the crowds of people cheering. Glen bowed and smiled, bowed and smiled. He had on white cowboy boots that sparkled like his sequined shirt.

Molly tugged her foot. She pushed it. She pulled it. It did not move. Neither did the pony's. Would she be here forever? Would the parade move on without her?

CHAPTER 7

Rachel Saves the Day

Molly's toe was beginning to get numb! Her sneaker was getting smudged! Glen Cooper was still bowing.

Molly hated to call for help. She hated to let adults know she was in trouble. None of the other Scouts had ponies who stood on their feet.

Molly saw Rachel at the head of the parade. Right behind Glen Cooper. Rachel wasn't leading the parade, Glen was, but she was close.

Just when Molly felt tears coming to her eyes, Rachel turned around and noticed

Molly's problem. She got down off her pony and came over to her.

"Don't worry," said Rachel. "I'll get him off."

And she leaned up against the pony's front leg and gave him a big shove. Up went his foot! Molly pulled her foot out quickly.

Molly wanted to throw her arms around Rachel and hug her. How could Molly ever have thought Rachel was selfish? She was the only one who saw Molly's problem. The only one who came and helped.

"Thank you," said Molly. "I didn't know what to do."

"They like to do that," said Rachel. "But all you have to do is give them a poke." Then she went back to her own pony and mounted him.

Molly felt so good about getting her foot back that she knew she could get on this pony without help. She crossed her fingers and said "Star light" again and put one foot in the stirrup. She threw her other leg over the way she'd been shown. She landed in the saddle!

She was actually on a horse! She wasn't falling off! She felt tall and proud. She could see the whole park from up here! Almost as far as the fairgrounds.

A clown came by and held on to the reins and saddle, and gave her pony a sugar lump.

"His name is Pal," said the clown.

Was the clown joking? Could you believe a clown? Did they say real things that were not funny sometimes?

"It's a nice name," she said, patting Pal on his thick neck.

This was fun. Molly wished she could stay on her pony forever. But what about when Pal moved?

People were gathering in the park now, to watch the parade begin. People lined both sides of the street for as far as Molly could see. Ropes blocked Main Street and the cars had to go another way.

Suddenly the music began and Glen shouted, "Here we go!"

Molly had goose bumps, it was so exciting. Like her first ride on a merry-go-round when she was little. Scary but fun.

The horses and ponies pranced in place and swished their tails to chase away the flies. Then just as they moved ahead into the cheering throng, there was a bloodcurdling scream!

It must be Sonny, thought Molly.

But it wasn't Sonny, it was Roger!

"Get me off of this thing!" he shouted. "This horse is hitting me with his tail!"

Roger tried to scramble off and tumbled into the arms of the helpers.

Now the crowd was laughing.

"Roger's pony swished his tail too high and it hit Roger's head," said Mary Beth, turning around to talk to Molly.

Roger's dad was trying to get Roger back on the pony, but Roger kicked and screamed and said no. Roger's pony walked along without a rider.

Glen Cooper was throwing candy to the children in the crowd.

People on the curbs were waving American flags.

Molly held on to the saddle with one hand, and waved with the other.

Behind the Pee Wees were marching bands and big fancy floats. Rodeo princesses rode on the floats wearing red-white-and-blue dresses.

Down Main Street wound the parade. At one corner the parade slowed down. Sonny's pony did not want to slow down. "Whoa!" called Sonny. But it was too late. Sonny's pony reared and pawed the air with his front feet. The helpers held the reins but still Sonny slid to the ground! His pony did not want Sonny to get back on him.

"There's another horse with no rider!" said Kevin, laughing.

But Pal pranced along as smoothly as could be, lifting his feet high and light. Molly did not remember when she had had such a good time. When they came to the end of the route, she did not want to get off. Everyone else had dismounted, and Molly clung to the saddle. She was the last one on her pony, and the last one off.

"Oh, my legs feel funny!" said Lisa. "It feels funny to walk again!"

After the parade, people wandered around the grounds, shaking Glen's hand, looking at the horses, and playing games and eating hot dogs with mustard.

When it began to grow dark, everyone gathered in the park for fireworks. Colored lights lit up the sky. They fell like a waterfall to the ground.

"Ooooh" and "Ahhh," said the people.

"This is the best Fourth of July I ever had," said Molly to Mary Beth.

"You worried for nothing," said Mary Beth. "You were the best rider of all."

The next Tuesday, the Pee Wee Scouts got their badges. Even Roger and Sonny got a badge.

"They rode their ponies," said Mrs. Peters. "For a shorter time."

"And now," said Mrs. Peters when all the badges had been passed out, "maybe Molly can tell us those good deeds she wanted to report."

Molly jumped. Why was Mrs. Peters asking for good deeds now? This wasn't a regular meeting! This was just a meeting to get their badges!

"Molly?" said their leader.

Molly wrinkled her forehead. She tried to think of her rhyming clues. *Cake, bake, rake, break.* But what did *break* have to do with her good deed?

"I didn't break any dishes when I dried them," she blurted out.

The Pee Wees laughed and laughed. "No one does," said Lisa.

Molly laughed too. She didn't care if she forgot. She'd think of it next time. Or she would do some new good deeds.

The important thing was, she rode a horse. Well, a pony. She stayed on it when Roger and Sonny did not. She may have been the best rider of all, as Mary Beth had said. And she had got her horse badge.

Rat's knees, she had worried about the wrong thing the whole time! What she had worried about hadn't happened! She would have to remember that next time.

Pee Wee Scout Song
(to the tune of
"Old MacDonald Had a Farm")

Scouts are helpers, Scouts have fun
Pee Wee, Pee Wee Scouts!
We sing and play when work is done,
Pee Wee, Pee Wee Scouts!

With a good deed here,
And an errand there,
Here a hand, there a hand,
Everywhere a good hand.

Scouts are helpers, Scouts have fun,
Pee Wee, Pee Wee Scouts!

Pee Wee Scout Pledge

We love our country
And our home,
Our school and neighbors too.

As Pee Wee Scouts
We pledge our best
In everything we do.